tellwell ✍

Tellwell Talent
www.tellwell.ca

ISBN
978-0-2288-8139-1 (Hardcover)
978-0-2288-8138-4 (Paperback)
978-0-2288-8140-7 (eBook)

My
Euphoric
Rose

MIGUELINA RAMIREZ

Edited by Katie Beaton

This book is dedicated to my loved ones and poetic readers who believe in my art.

May you shine your bright light!

TABLE OF CONTENTS

SUN

ROSE

MOON

SUN

OUR LIVES

travelled to the mountains
to spend time with you
inhaled the mighty breeze
and exhaled the stress of the city
we nestled between the fireplace
drinking hot cocoa
I looked up at your sweet face
and knew this was the life
that I wanted

Miguelina Ramirez

THANK THE EARTH

as the sun's rays coat my bare face

the mellow atmosphere fills with Love and Light

I feel the euphoric high of life in this moment

and the sense of living my life with purpose

life is so beautiful, but not many

get to enjoy or experience its vibrations

I humble my thoughts

I thank the earth

I shower my emotions with gratitude

I make every day count

for I have a purpose in this life

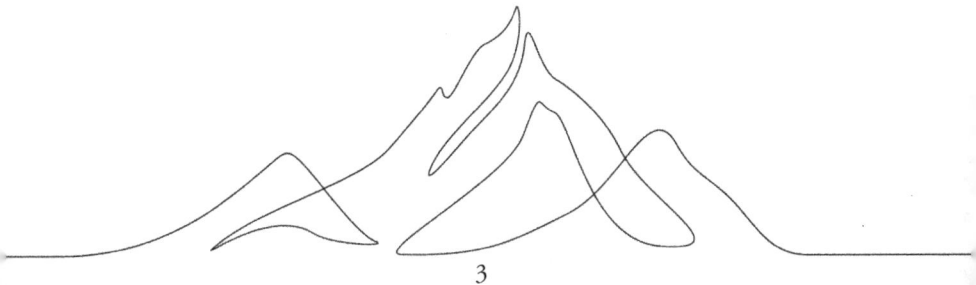

PURPOSE

as I surround myself

with the warmth

of my loved ones

a sense of purpose fills the room

I want to make it for them

make them proud

and fill their lives

with the riches of the world

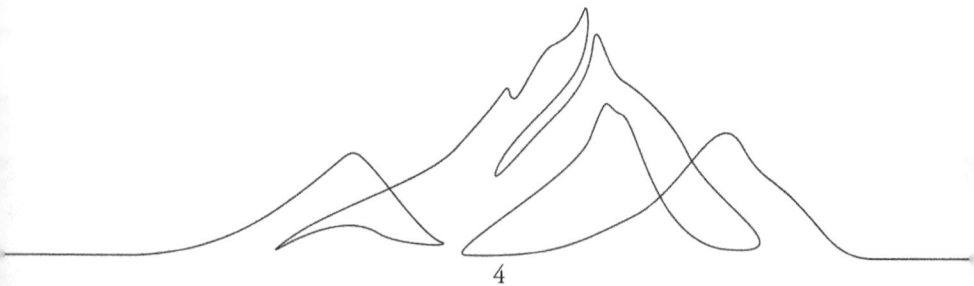

REFLECTION

I know
I'm on the path
I must follow

GRAINS OF RICE

opportunities are like

grains of rice

by the thousands

they present themselves

how you choose to cook them

is entirely up to you

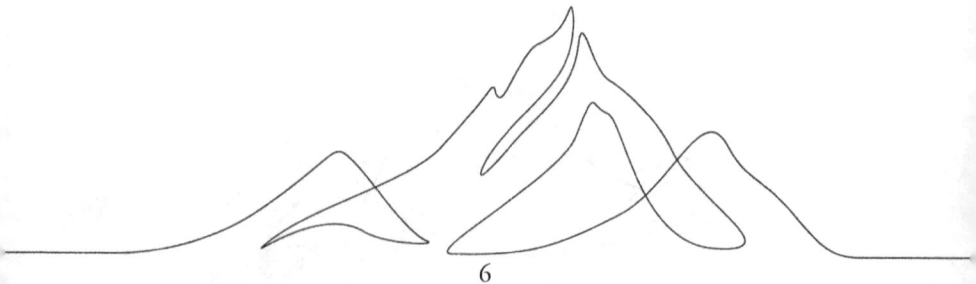

NOT FOR YOU

sometimes you have to close

a door

to open a window

knowing when something is

not for you

and knowing when to

let go

is an achievement

within itself

ALIGNMENT

your talents are not out of alignment

with your journey

if you stumble in rocky waters

you alone have to manage

your energy

and time will follow

patience is a virtue

a virtue that is often taken for granted

THE BALANCE

we must work to live

and not live to work

for the time we have on this earth is valuable

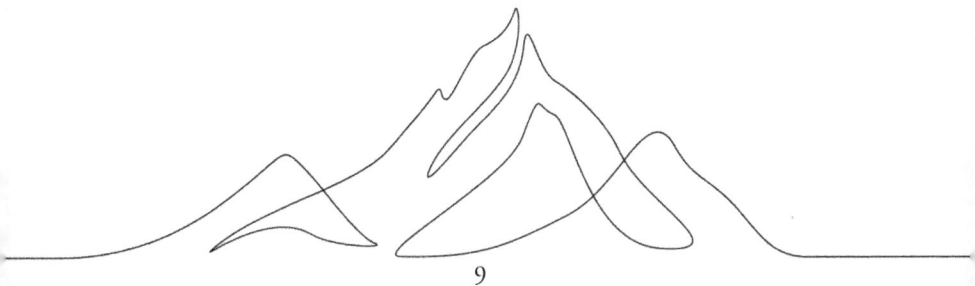

ONE LIFE

a world full of endless possibilities

the world is your oyster

do what you love

and love what you do

DIVINE

red-stained lips, dark brown hair

how she moves like the wind

smoothly and gracefully

how she smiles like the sun

warm and bright

how she doesn't show her sorrows or losses

mighty, filled with wisdom and experience

and how she carries the world on her shoulders

I applaud her for that

PAINTER

she often paints with her fingertips

soaking in pastel blues

she motions her fingers

side to side

ever so swift

she stands back and observes

the masterpiece that

she has created

humming to her thoughts

she is content

DANCE

there's something truly magical
in movement

allowing your body to be free
without judgement
letting the rhythm
take over

being present with spirit is
such a healing experience

EVERGREEN

evergreen
ever blue
you love the earth
and the soil beneath your feet

the environment has always been your forte
you see past
materialistic crap and fancy lifestyles
you'd rather live in the forest or the mountains

and I think that's refreshing, love

UNAPOLOGETICALLY YOU

you coat your face with glitter

shimmering in different colours

you know your truths

your world, your mind, and your time

are all that matter to you

for you are unapologetically you

HEAVENLY

you are miraculous, brighter than all the stars

translucent

transcending through space

you are radiant

absorbing the sun's rays

you are whole like the moon above

with your godlike features

you are glory

ARMS

the best feeling is embracing you in my arms

TIME

it's never too late

to find the person you're destined to be

allow time to heal all wounds

my sweet angel

TO BE

to be loved deeply

to be wanted mentally

to be embraced into your cozy arms physically

to be yours spiritually

to be your life partner

HUMMINGBIRD

my spirit animal, so free and so elegant

you are like no other

I catch a glimpse of you, now and then

as you make your daily debut

I know I am on the path I must follow

I hum to the sight of your presence

for I know you are a significant part of me

I AM

I am the light this world needs

I am kind, I am wise

I am blessed, I am me

BODY

it took a minute for me to love you

you house my soul, my mind, and my wisdom

you keep me warm, you never take what isn't yours

you have battle scars and stretch marks that make you

unique

thank you, body

for loving me

INTROVERT

she clinched her books as she walked past the busy school hallways

how she dreaded making eye contact with the other students

but it wasn't the anxiety that was holding her back

she knew if she made eye contact

with that one person

they would see her

not her physical self

but her soul

and she wasn't ready to let anybody in

PEI

your familiar voice reminds me of
the PEI summer breeze
warm and tangy
yet sturdy and swift
the summers are always delightful
in Prince Edward Island

COTTON CLOUDS

cotton candy fills the night sky

pink

blue

purple

and navy dance the night away

vibrant colours shimmer over the horizon

these are the moments

I cherish the most

thank you, Mother Earth

for letting time stand still in this moment

SUMMER

the summers are kinder

to the young and the old

time doesn't seem to suppress their innocence

for the sun gives them energy

and the blue skies allow

daydreamers to inquire of a world

where they could fly

and harmony is in arm's reach

JOY

the Joy in things

Joy has brought me to where I am

Joy is kind and sweet

she understands the path I must be on

Joy is of Love and Light

she is full of wisdom

Joy is home to me

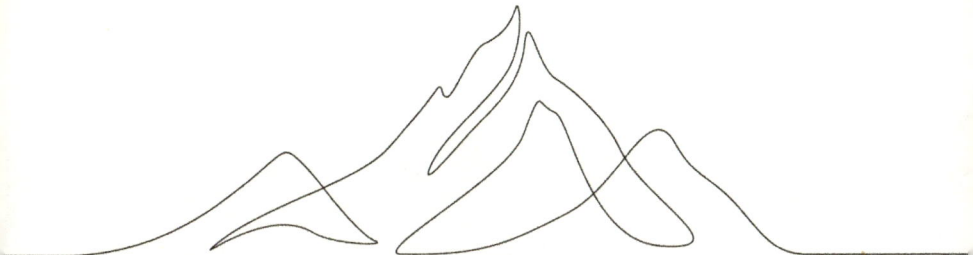

ETERNAL SUNSHINE

in the land of eternal sunshine
is where I find tranquillity
this fruitful, harmonious land
coated with the sun's mighty rays
true enlightenment lives here

PEACE OF MIND

when the sun shines through

the window panes

I'm reminded

that it'll all be okay

where there's light

there's love

and where there's love

there's light

SUNLIGHT

I coat myself in sunlight

I feel the everlasting warmth of the sun's rays

on my bare face

I am glorified

true enlightenment comes from within

LIFE

elegant and free, how the branches sway side to side

the autumn air meets the sunrise

black coffee and green tea make for a morning delight

you inhale nature's aroma and exhale the sweet nectar we call life

ALWAYS GROUNDED

skin and bones

you are greater than your human flesh

awakened and in tune with the vibrations of the earth, you are always grounded

EARTHY VIBRATIONS

you are a tall glass of water

refreshing to the taste

you quench my thirst

pure and holy

full of minerals and

earthy vibrations

I drink

BROWN SUGAR, HONEY, AND COCOA

your essence radiates, my love

brown sugar mixed with honey, you're pure as the milky way

your kind heart and the words you speak bring energy into my inner self

we vibrate

let's vibrate

your cocoa complexion was created by the great ones, my love

my queen

let's meditate and manifest this life into existence

LOVE & LIGHT

in our lives, I see kids and a happy home

I see successful careers and healthy relationships

I see bedtime stories and forehead kisses

a sizeable amount of laughter

and so much love

for kindness is our mantra in our household

the balance in things makes everything right

Miguelina Ramirez

BRANCHES

we are only fragments
connected by the tree of life
where its mighty branches
stretches from far and wide

WONDERFUL WORLD

I often live in my present state
fantasizing on the past and future
suppresses my need for adventure

in the now
I wish to experience
the wonderful world around me
to breath and to feel liberated
to live in the present
it's all I have

PULSE

nothing is more important
than your beating pulse
your breathing glorifies my inner aura
I am your maker

Miguelina Ramirez

JUST BREATHE

inhale

exhale

repeat

ROSE

PARK BRAKE

subside any feelings
you may hold and release
the park brake that
held you
motionless all your life

HOPE

we moved in the night with nothing

but our hopes and dreams

strapped to our ankles

tiptoeing

through the fields

carrying our bravery, courage, and wisdom on our backs

to save the generation that follows

hearing the echoes

the cries

the pain, we endured

when we were enslaved

in the mind of our enemies

SHIELD

you bury your emotion underneath the soil

so that it may never see the sunlight

and so that others may never see your vulnerable side

I found a crack in the foundation

and I watered you until

you sprouted

Miguelina Ramirez

MIGHTY HANDS

I know you need healing
you've been searching all your life
for the one with the mighty hands
that could fix the impurities
and imperfections that make you
insecure
healing starts within
and within starts the healing

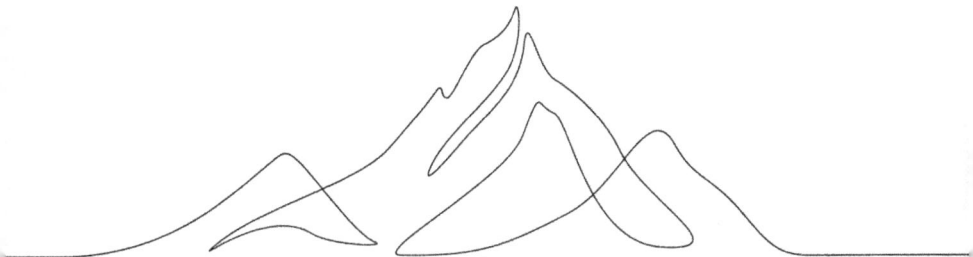

HURT

I can tell you have been hurt before

you let the drugs numb your pain
you let it fill the void
your actions speak louder than words

I can't take your pain away
but I can be there on your lonely nights
I can embrace the man you are
I can hold you tight at night

you see, I have been hurt before
I have experienced such sadness
but it made me the person I am today, with a little sacrifice

so, I'll water you
you water me
we will grow together?

EX-LOVER

you carry your past trauma

so well and hide it in between the cracks of your smile

she broke a piece of you

that you can't quite comprehend

the emotions that you keep hidden

your future lovers can't break through the thick layers

that keep you introverted

with your lonely thoughts

to move on

you must forgive your past lover

and accept that time heals all wounds

heartbreaks come and go

it's in what is learned

that we grow

WILDFLOWER

I want to make you happy

mentally

spiritually and physically

you bloom through all the obstacles

and shine through the struggles

you wear your heart on your sleeve

you're a wildflower mixed with courage and perseverance

your essence radiates

my love

NEW BEGINNINGS

as the kettle starts to hiss and rattle

the clock ticks, time moves

and you are no longer the old you

allow yourself to heal

accept that life is worth living

for you are more than you realize

my dear

BIRD

endangered bird, you are rare and graceful

for there is not many of your kind around

LIGHTHOUSE

your eyes carry a healing light to those you encounter

FLIGHT

took a plane
to visit you today
how I missed your touch
your smell
your laugh
separated by
the different time zones
and the many miles
we count down the hours
until
we embrace
no length of time or distance
can break the love we have
for each other

we sacrifice
our present time
so that we don't
sacrifice the
precious moments
later

we work our twenties away
so that we may
grow in our thirties
and forties

as we board our plane
and ascend into space
wide-eyed and content
I feel a beam of euphoria
and excitement
to finally move from this
draining town is liberating
to the spirit body

SUITCASE

you embarked on my misty thoughts

full of hope and opportunity

you followed the journey

we left with nothing but a suitcase

full of ambition

VOYAGERS

we were voyagers, set out on a path to find enlightenment

we travelled through many valleys and the roughest water

turned down the brightest diamonds and the purest gold

the path was not to find materialistic riches but to find peace within the bodies that house our souls

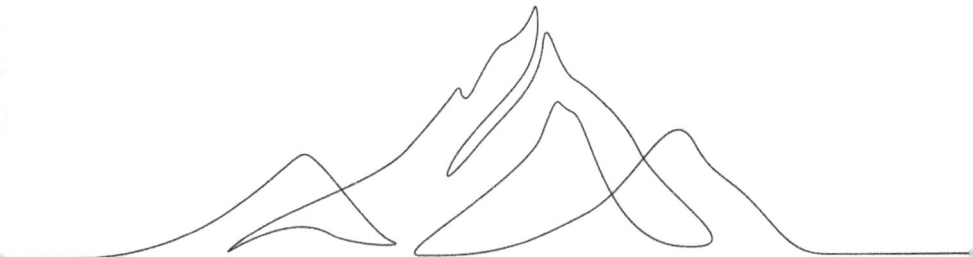

WIFE

to be loved by you in this lifetime

to be the woman you have always prayed for

to be wanted by your touch

to be the one who makes you laugh

to be your wife one day

LOVE

love is all we need to heal this hurting planet

THE HEALING

many people are trying to heal

while trying to feel

and trying to feel

while trying to heal

it's in

what you choose

in this lifetime

that matters

MATURITY

choosing what we do with our

traumatic life experiences

stabilizing the chemicals that make us human

and defusing certain situations with our actions

equals growth and validation

being the mature person

does have its rewards in this fiesta

we call life

we are spiritual beings living a human life

and that's okay

GROWTH

protect your energy

get rid of the things

that don't serve you in this lifetime

ESSENTIAL STEP

forgiveness doesn't always come easy

when trying to heal the mind, body, and spirit

forgiveness takes growth, patience, and acceptance

it is an essential step

in healing

VIBRATIONS

to heal oneself spiritually,

connect to the vibrations

of the earth

and allow time

to just be

Miguelina Ramirez

A MAN AND HIS BIKE

he biked until his legs were shaking

and knees where hurting

he biked halfway across the country

to find liberation within himself

he was lost but found his footing along the way

the road was windy and weary

the reward was greater than life itself

peace and abundance greeted him at his final destination

THE GIFT OF LIVING

the gift of living
is choosing to live such a
peaceful and honest life

STITCHES

specks of water fall onto my windowpane

in early May,

the fresh smell of lemongrass and the warm sun rays

allow time to pass and wounds to heal

but when you came around

the stitches came undone

my inner thoughts spilled out into

a greater depression of self-doubt and hopelessness

it was my angels

who stitched me up

as time began to pass again

Miguelina Ramirez

GROWING PAINS

a single tear falls from my eyes

my tongue tastes the salt

I am reminded of how far I've come

and how this is only transient

in my expedition to equanimity

WAITING

I was waiting for you

when I should have been waiting

for myself

to heal my past wounds

you were just the salt

to make it sting

WELDER

how am I supposed to heal

when there's nothing left to mend?

I have welded my heart too many times

forged it in the fire

coated it with heavy protectant

yet, you still manage to get through

and shatter it into a million pieces

COLD

like a block of ice
you chiselled at me with an ice pick
violently shaken
I peel back the layers
that have made me insensitive
all these years

RENEWAL

submerging myself underwater

and allowing my sins to depreciate off me

like a baptism

I was cleansed of all wrongdoings

and rebirthed into a better me

Miguelina Ramirez

ELEGANT WINGS

I make sacrifices

is that what life is?

like an earthworm

I ascended into a

translucent butterfly

spread my elegant wings

and flew

STRANGERS

beautiful people

walk hand in hand

I am surrounded by strangers

yet there's something truly magical and mystical

in all these curious, wondering eyes

MUSE

what is a poet without their muse,

you may ask?

I find beauty in all creations

thoughts, feelings, and affirmations

2.22.22

more beautiful than any rose

your essence radiates

we cherish the moments that we are given

POET

you caught the sail of my arc and tumbled into my existence

the nights seem almost unbearable

transcending through brails of emotions

I am not forgotten

a poet turns feelings into words

and words into emotions

you are my muse

EYES

your beaming eyes
cut through
the pillars of life
I know I'm where
I need to be

SILK PRESS

the silk press binds and folds thousands of silks

to produce a single garment

the stitches that are carefully placed

form the foundation

that coat your silhouette

sits ever so gracefully on your collar bones

you are alluring to my sight

DIAMOND

the beauty that you possess doesn't even comprehend the word

greatness

for you are greater than all the greats

shining so bright, the stars are jealous of your beauty

your sweet lips and dazzling eyes

are heavenly

so captivating to the eyes

for I know beauty fades

but this love will never die

you are more precious than gold

you are my diamond among the rocks

RARE

you are a rare flower with petals

so delicate and fragile

that the earth vibrates

when you bloom

my love

HUNGER

a utopia of violet shimmer coats tonight's sky

breathtaking to the senses, we indulge

tonight, we feast on the riches of the heavens

SCULPTOR

the sculptor met his cay

cool to the touch and smooth through his fingers

he created a masterpiece out of mud

molded and shaped, he did

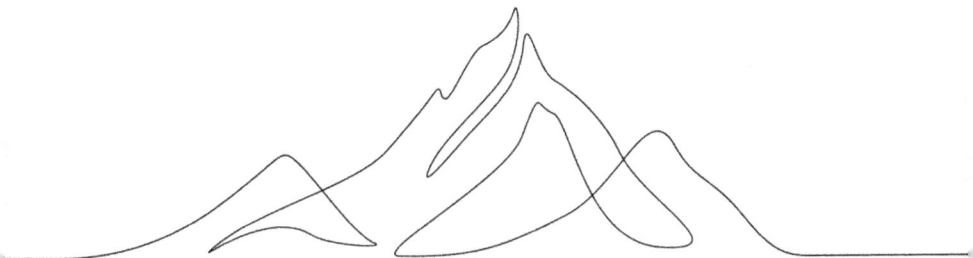

WINE

he turned water into wine

and wine into you

graceful, your lips appeal

what is romance without its poet?

and what is a poet without their muse?

you quench my thirst

MAGNET

mesmerized and magnetized by your golden aura

your soulful beauty and your piercing green eyes are violently breathtaking

your energy does not go unnoticed

ART

you treat your body as an art exhibit

only a few are welcome

and fewer can touch the fine art piece

MUSEUM

you are a museum full of the finest art

for your soul holds the complexions of serenity

your aura dances to earth's vibrations

and those soulful eyes beam the violet flame

you are my astounding art piece

your beauty is perpetual

JOURNEY

millions of travellers

journey near and far

to appreciate art museums

I'd travel near and far to appreciate you

FEEL SOMETHING

art doesn't need to look alluring or pleasing

it's meant to make you feel something

you are art to me

RAIN

summer thunderstorms make their way

unto our horizon

the lightning crashes, the sky rumbles

you pause and look at me

no words being spoken as your gaze falls into

my inner soul

it's heavily raining and I've never felt this deep soulful connection
before

only if you knew how you made me feel that night

LOVELY BONES

we spent the night

embraced in each other's arms

as the hours pressed on

we listened to the echoing silence

no words being spoken

I could hear his inner thoughts

and I was hoping this night wouldn't end

he kissed my boney spine

I kissed his soft hands

overwhelmed by how perfect we were for each other

he saw the light in my eyes

I felt the kindness on his lips

a euphoric high ascended

Miguelina Ramirez

WONDERING EYES

as the night passes through

time stands still

our eyes intertwine

you feed my inner soul

to hold this euphoric feeling

is causing a great ordeal

my love

Miguelina Ramirez

HOME

you came out of nowhere and rocked my world

you are like no other

rare as they come, you listen to my inner thoughts

you see me for me, and I thank you for that

I found a home in your arms and made a bed on your chest

your forehead kisses assure me that you're here to stay

FREQUENCY

therapeutic conversations

long car rides home

we hum to the different

radio channels

laughter fills

the atmosphere

as we make our

way home

LIPS

the taste of your lips

sends radio waves

into my chakras

HOW YOU MAKE ME FEEL

your favourite song is
how you make me feel
the vibe is impeccable
and the feeling is ecstatic

Miguelina Ramirez

MUSIC TO MY EARS

when I look at you

the orchestra plays in my mind

the sound of your voice is liberating

to the senses

no words can express my gratitude

for your kind eyes

darling, I just want to dance

with you

Miguelina Ramirez

TALL GRASS

we can leave right now
just say the word
and I'm yours
take me to another place
where we can be ourselves
where the grass is long
and the swaying trees
cover our bodies
I will always follow
you're all I need
in this lifetime

FLAME

if words could describe

how you make me feel

the words would dance right off this page

into a euphoric galaxy far away

for you are my violet light

shining divinely bright

making all the stars in tonight's sky

jealous of your flame

SAFE

fingers intertwined
lips met ears
you whispered,
let down your guard
you're safe in my arms

YOURS

awaken the woman in me
squeeze the palms of my hands
run your fingers down my spine
whisper that I am yours

Miguelina Ramirez

WHOLE

when sparks fly and our tongues meet
we are more than skin and bones
our energies become one

TOUCH

you feel like home

to me

FOUNDATION

freshly cut roses lay ever so gently on the kitchen counter

our mornings are filled with forehead kisses and the smell of freshly-made cookies

we have created a beautiful life together

laughter fills the hollow space that connects the foundation

we have created a beautiful home

LIFE PARTNER

they talk about our love in movies and novels

I am the air

he is the lungs, inhaling my sweet breeze

home he is to me

time stands still when I am in his elegant presence

for we are young and in love

his sweet lips quench my thirst

I know our love is pure

PRECIOUS MOMENTS

an art major, he was

full of mystery and wonder

he embraced me in his longing arms

separated, with what little time we had

we made every moment count

ANGEL

sweeter than sugar and more precious than gold

she's the spitting image of our love

she chooses us and I'm forever grateful

melanin skin

rosy cheeks and

curious wondering eyes

bring sunshine into our hectic lives

LOVING YOU

loving you has filled my empty cup,

you fulfill me

you bring sunshine into my cloudy life

a breath of fresh air is nothing compared to the love we share

you are my soulmate

you make my soul vibrate

the universe knew how perfectly imperfect this love would be

I will find you in the next life

Miguelina Ramirez

MY OTHER HALF

no length of time apart

can break this everlasting bond

birthed and nurtured throughout the years

I am the soil

you are the earth, allowing me to be

FOREVER

a place in my life where I could breathe

and be free

my everlasting home

is with you

UNCONDITIONAL

as you press your stubby beard against my forehead

eyes closed and content

I feel the warmth from your lips touches my bare skin

a wide grin fills my face

I am reminded of how love truly is unconditional

KEY

my theme in life is love

I surround my thoughts

my emotions

my intentions

with this powerful affirmation

for it is the key to life

SEARCHING

we are all searching for love
when love is simply in all of us
love is in the eyes
of my mother braiding my hair
love is on the lips
of my nephew calling my name
love hides in between
the hellos and the goodbyes
love is patient and always kind

BRIGHT LIGHT

we've walked a very long path together

only to meet again in this lifetime

you are radiant and transparent

your smile lights up the darkest room

a true friend

a rare friend

you love deeply

may you continue to shine

your bright light

SUNSHINE

watching you grow into

the man you are today

brings sunshine into my existence

we shared similar life

experiences

overcame

the high and lows of it

we continued to

preserve the memories

that humbled us

there's nothing I wouldn't do

for you

little brother

UNCONDITIONAL COMPANION

as I listen to your inner vibrations

I am reminded of how beautiful life truly is

how peaceful and vibrant you make my life

my unconditional companion

so gentle and sweet you are to me

you see what others don't

and hear my deepest thoughts

you stare and nod to my silly talks with your curious eyes

you love every part of me

my unconditional companion

please walk this road with me

FRIEND

she coats herself in laughter

her enormous heart paints a beautiful

transcending rainbow

her smile is heavenly to the sight

for she is captivating and graceful

LIBERATION

love unconditionally liberates

the mind

spirit

and body

to love and feel this endearment

is truly magical

love heals the inner wounds

and feeds the soul body

ANTIDOTE

when your heart hurts

mine does too

and when the pain

gets too unbearable

my lips will

be the antidote

to your suffering

EMPATH

hopeless romantic, I am
the feelings just seem to get deeper
and deeper like a spiralling staircase
I make my presence known
loving you is the best part of me
absorbing the euphoric highs
and lows is just the process

WAVELENGTHS

sharing the same vibrational wavelength as your partner

is truly breathtaking

he howls at my quirkiness

I chuckle at his jokes

we just make it work

SOUL HARMONY

our physical bodies were strangers

but our souls were in tune and connected in some way

LOVE LANGUAGE

she is the only woman I would wait for

her inner beauty is pure to the core

she embodies independence

with her gentle touch and demeanour, she is transparent

she loves with her heart and speaks with her mind

she is the definition of a strong Black woman

serenity, she moves with such grace

Black excellence, my queen

what's your love language?

Miguelina Ramirez

HOUSE PLANT

our love is like a plant

shy and witty at first

yet mighty and strong

it flourishes

we bath in love, patience, and honesty

and as we learn about each other's thoughts

a seed is rooted

with time and loyalty, we grow

Miguelina Ramirez

TRUE

I can see your
fluorescent colours
appearing
with the wind in your hair
and the sun
beaming effortlessly on you
your essence is radiant
and your true self
resonates with my aura

ENERGY

you are mighty

you play roles that not many can comprehend

you are the balance and the answers

that I've been searching for

SENSES

you feed my senses

my mouth waters at your intelligence

INTIMACY

to be

touched

admired

adored

the uncontrollable need for your sights to be on me

to be compatible with your inner self

to be loved by you

in this lifetime

23

you watched the sunset as I watched your eyes

set upon tonight's beautiful sky

our favourite pastime is to watch

Mother Earth's aura dance so effortlessly

with your hands in mine

and my head on your chest

you make me feel enlightened

this is how Juliet felt in the arms of Romeo

for you are my Romeo

and my love for you will never depreciate

my love for you is eternal

PAST LIFE

the sun's going down
and the colours are just breathtaking
you are my heaven on earth
we must have known each other in a past life
for this feels so natural, so right
I found the man of my dreams
warm and gentle he is to me

Miguelina Ramirez

LOVE AFFAIR

our love affair

glances to the moon

for the moon sees our rendezvous

and late-night strolls

we are lovers connected only by touch

that very touch that makes me feel

as though the earth would quake

if you left

Miguelina Ramirez

BUTTERFLIES

I kiss you so gently
so that you may feel
my beating pulse in your arms
you give me butterflies
and as the moon shines through
I am reminded
of how innocent
our love affair is

MOON

IMPERFECT TIMING

as swiftly as the waves crashed against the shoreline

you ascended into my life unpredictably

our eyes interlocked

I touched your beating pulse

you felt like home to me

our lively conversations

our midnight strolls

were just an illusion in our faint reality

for you had other plans

realism crept in

and our fairy-tale romance expired

CIRCLES

drawing circles

connecting the dots

until we meet

again

you spin me round

and round

and you press your fingers to my lips

and you whisper,

I'm your protector

SMALL

laughing at your jokes again
I'm always making myself feel small
so that I can fit
into the palm of your hands

you cradle my thoughts and emotions
in your longing arms

like a merry-go-round
in slow motion
I'm always losing myself
in your eyes

Miguelina Ramirez

PUZZLE PIECE

tomorrow is a new day

to start again

trying to fit the adjacent pieces

into this uncompromising

puzzle game

is tearing us apart

BETRAYAL

don't hurt me again
I have kept myself
small for you
so that there was
enough room
for the both of us

SPACE

I thought I knew what love was
until you told me you needed space
as though the thought of me
made you question my existence in your life
you needed a way out, a clean break
I was propelling over your mind constantly
and when the sound of my voice
met your longing ears
you knew that distance and time
were the only antidote
to subside any feelings lingering around your aura
you wanted space
but I needed closure

FADE

what is distance

if being in your presence is dreadful?

what is pain

if you self-sabotage?

what is the point?

if we are not happy in this relationship

why ponder?

if our love has depreciated

slowly release me

gently let our love fade

UNFAITHFUL

she gave me a family to love

a family to hold

I took it for granted

made a bed out of despair

and slept in it

like a baby

GOOD DAYS

cherry blossom candles

relaxing R&B music and a glass of white wine

on these lonely nights

I've been working too hard and too long to settle for your half-cut apologies

you can't hold my heart and expect me to wait for you

TEDDY BEAR

you gave me comfort
like my childhood teddy bear
I hugged you
a little too tightly

but you wasted my time
and when I saw the signs
I should have let you go
but I held on
knowing that the pleasure was greater
than the pain
I was going to endure

BRIDGE

we were meant to build a bridge to the everlasting vessel of our love

you chose her

and the lavender essence of your smell fades

from my empty cage of hurt and self-doubt

you are no longer somebody to me

THE BREAKUP

if this relationship was erased

we both would have been happier

I was able to breathe the moment

you let me go

like it was fresh air

I gave you the time of day and you gave me endless

excuses

PANDORA

a roller coaster of emotions

you have opened Pandora's box

from lovers to strangers

you have chiselled your way out of my life

I have installed roadblocks and handrails

around my shivering heart

to protect what is left

from your unpleasant attendance

to your game of cards

Miguelina Ramirez

VIOLIN

you played my heart

like a living violin

and then you plucked the strings out

when you were finished

with your recital

SELFISH

you're losing your wife
your marriage is ending
losing your self-control
is the least of your problems
I am not the women that has caused
your broken home
your chapter was already coming to an end
before you caught my sight
you were selfish
I was naïve
and all she needed
was a reason to leave

Miguelina Ramirez

BRUISES

the markings on your surface are

clearer than day

you'd rather chip your pride

than swallow

the bitter pill

we call reality

EYES CLOSED

the hate you give moves the sea

for you are lightning and thunder

when you aren't pleased

the moon can't control the tides that rock your life

you are afloat

you made a home out of despair and weakness

for toxicity rules your mind

DARKNESS

he doesn't fear death
for death is always at his door
he has lost so much
and lost himself
in the process
the pillars of life took
him by the horns
and mended him into
chaos
he now lives deep in his thoughts
away from human interactions
and with his sins
which are like corpses
he prays for saving

IMPRINT

you were imprinted on my heart
showing me your rarest parts

yet you took me for granted
making me feel broken and belittled
yet I still had so much love for you

and even though the strings
which once made me feel whole
are slowing breaking off
I still mask my feelings

ATTACHMENTS

seeking validation in the eyes of the men

who belittled us

searching for emotional attachments to fill

the emptiness that just can't be filled

with lust, gifts, and material things

spending many nights deep in thought

wondering why being sad is comforting

and being happy

is just a temporary illusion

that feels unfamiliar

Miguelina Ramirez

COWBOY

you lasso my emotions, like a cowboy

whipping his rope around a cow's neck

I beg,

set me free!

the chaos fills the room

as I'm slowly losing my breath,

I find tranquillity

in between the chaos and commotion

and that's when I finally grasp

that the rope will set me free

TOXICITY

I will not let myself
fall back into your arms, I have grown
without you by my side
my mind, body, and soul
have flourished, without your cold touch
I will not let my heart
take any more of the misery
you have caused when you decided
to walk away

DRAIN

dating you

was like jumping off a cliff to liberation

misty, exciting

suffocating your lovers

was all you knew

draining their energies with pointless arguments

was your expertise

but I loved how complicated you were

I thought I could fix you,

fix us

BOTTLE

I have bottled up the feelings

that you gave to me

until my future lover

will find it stranded beneath

the grains of sand

DATING

dating in the city is fast-paced

an emotionless whirling wave

we pretend

with nothing but the best intentions

nobody wants to waste their time

more importantly, nobody wants to

end up alone

so, we pretend

through dinner and cocktails

that we're living the lustful life we wanted

but we don't need it

ONLY IF

the choices we'll make

the people we'll meet

the places we'll go

and the stories we'll tell

if you give our love a chance

STAY

it's you
it's always been you
as the smell of vanilla fills the room
the Christmas air makes its presence known
I was thinking of my past lovers
when I knew my future was in your hands
I told you to leave
when I wanted you to stay
you should've just
stayed

ONE THAT GOT AWAY

you ask my friends how I've been lately

how the years have treated my kind heart

and about the lucky man that has cherished my soul

I was indeed the one that got away

I live in your fading

memories and it's slowly

crippling you

WEARY NIGHTS

you keep

me close

so that you may never forget

our weary nights

DROWNING

as I'm slowly drowning

in the deep

I see the sunlight

piercing through the water

I'm calm and accepting

of my fate before the gates of heaven open

and before I'm greeted by

my deceased family members

a hand reaches in and pulls me out

a stranger has rescued me

from the public swimming pool

I was five years old

this memory

lingers into my present self

I have always felt close to my angels ever since that day

EMBRACED

as my birth mother

embraced me in her warm arms

I felt a sense of home

no words can express

the emotions

that brought me back to

my euphoric childhood state

MANGO TREE

faint childhood memories linger as I stare up into space

I wonder how that mango tree is holding up after all these years

scraped knees and achy arms

we didn't care, we were kids back then

how I loved to climb that mango tree

faint memories creep in when we least expect them to

Miguelina Ramirez

INNOCENCE

grass-stained blue jeans
ketchup-stained tank tops
a smile worth a thousand
words
the park is where we met
the summers were filled
with endless laughter
the innocence in our youth
brings appreciation
into my now busy
adult life

ADDICTION

garden of my youth, the gentle unfolding of our souls

making a fort out of our misfortunes

and building a home in each other's arms

you are what I crave

ETERNAL YOUTH

to be nineteen again

to jump through the seasons

like it was nothing

to drink

like it was nothing

to feel invisible and liberated

yet feel the whole world on my shoulders

the sweet breeze in my tangled hair

and the long car rides back to you

my eternal youth

YOUNG LOVERS

you saw the potential in my eyes and knew I was going places

you quietly observed and kept your distance

almost a decade later

I close my eyes and picture the life that we could have had together

the kids we could've raised together

the places we could've travelled together

for I smile at the thought of the could have, should have

we're living in completely different cities with our life partners

living completely different lives

I wonder to this day if you think of us

MEMORIES

the memories that I cherish

do age like a glass of fine wine

on a summer's night

I pause and grin at the mental sight of your vivid half-smile

as faint as the memories protrude

the longing for your touch feels as though

time would stand still

if I ever saw your kind eyes again

NEEDED YOU

standing at the edge of the driveway

I waited

for your kind eyes to meet me

you played our favourite record

we reminisced about our time

together

filled with nothing

but love

my safe haven

was in your arms

and I will continue to wait

if it means dancing with you

one last time

Miguelina Ramirez

RACE MY MIND

we reminisce on our fast-paced relationship
we both wanted to feel
the wind in our hair
the beach salt on our longing arms
the sand pressed between our toes
we were both young and in love
dancing many nights away
stumbling into bars
in our twenties
and singing to our songs
it was a lust for life
a lust for us
filled with nothing but the best
memories
of our time together

Miguelina Ramirez

JUNGLE

she's from the jungle

coated with the earth's vibrations

she often sings

I call her my sugar cane

others call her

the plantain queen

she comes in many forms

and holds the

fruit-bearing seeds

WOMANHOOD

as the spatter of blood
coats the bathroom floor
a sharp pain makes its presence known
I have entered into womanhood

as the flow of rich blood
runs down my thighs
I am overcome with revelation and perplexity

how magical
how sacred
the woman's temple
truly is

MAKE IT OUT

we found each other
in a broken place
shattered pieces of glass beneath our feet

we lived in a community
where "hurt people" hurt people
it was a never-ending cycle of despair and with
no way out

not only did the men in our lives
treat us like puppets
but life seemed worthless
no liberation

you were different
you saw the potential
the hope
and the love in my eyes
and you knew
you had to make it out
for us

BATTLING THE TIDES

the mighty wave currents

pull us in

swallows me whole

you're slowly losing the battle

with the tides

you must

keep fighting

Miguelina Ramirez

ENSLAVED

bound

by metal shackles

and chains

we must chose our

words carefully

Miguelina Ramirez

SUBSTANCES

numbing the pain
with these foreign substances
is killing you inside
feeling the synthetic euphoria
is all you know
it brings you comfort
while creating a misty cloud around your aura
you indulge in the sadness
and it keeps you trapped

MISHANDLED

I mishandled my thoughts, emotions, and body
when I decided to let you back into my life
addiction is not always
a substance but an entity
pulling you in, spinning you around
like a mighty wave current

INTRUDER

anxiety is a silent killer

living in between thin layers

of missed opportunities and chances

feeding off fear

housing the soul body behind bars

and lingering

until it finds its next host

Miguelina Ramirez

DARK

it's been weeks, no months

since I slept like a normal person

the darkness fills the room

I must let the light shine through

deep underneath my covers, I overthink

if I just wait until daylight breaks

I can sleep

in peace

without judgement

so I wait

GREY

waves of grey sway side to side

something died inside of you

when you found out

everything is now changing

when hearts intertwine

they call it true love

and when a loved one departs

they call it grief

I will eternally celebrate

your beautiful life

Miguelina Ramirez

GENERATIONS

timeless, your beauty quenches generations

SKIES

mellow skies

accede into our horizons

the wave crashes

the birds echo

the trees sway

the sun finds its

beating rest

the moon appears

as I'm swaddled in my deep thoughts

I make my way home

Miguelina Ramirez

CATALYST

to suppress my emotions

is like holding my head

underwater and not allowing myself

to reach the shallow surface

GOODBYE

from stargazing lovers to strangers

our chapter has ended

REFUGE

a blanket of black velvet coats the night sky

awake and in tune with my thoughts

I often ponder on my past, present, and future self

how much I have grown as an individual suppresses

any negative thoughts

overcome with gratitude and clarity

for the lessons

I have learned along the way

led me to where I've assembled

my refuge

SILENCE

as I sit in this silence
I reflect on all my wonderful memories
and the blessings I have encountered
the taste of life is enriched with love
and the sweet nectar we call enlightenment

PEN & PAPER

tangled in my thoughts

I pull out a pen and paper

writing down my feelings has always been

therapeutic to my soul

I write until

my hand aches

and my back hurts

I find liberation

in between the soft-

ridged pages

MIDNIGHT THOUGHTS

midnight thoughts make their way
into our pillow talks
you pause and hesitate, the simplest words
start to form a linear cloud
swirling above your head, you debate
if your lips can share
overanalyzing was always your comfort zone
a big part of who you are
you cradle the thoughts like a Ferris wheel
in motion, only to meet my intuitive eyes
my lips, reassuring you that I'm here to stay

DEAR FRIEND

the pain that you carry is weighing you down

like a bag of bricks on your chest

you share with your close friends the burden that you feel

but that doesn't erase the pain and trauma you have experienced

you lay awake at night

fantasizing about how you could have found

your shivering voice

how badly you wanted to scream for help

how extremely low this individual made you feel

how you were only twelve years old

when you lost your mother

and you lost yourself

this pain lingers into your adulthood

but the monster who caused such sadness

has departed

and the pieces that once made you whole

are slowly mending themselves

and you wish to heal your mind

your spirit

your heart

in this lifetime

THE SHEDDING

surrender the feelings that you hold hostage and allow yourself to
shed the rigid layers that keeps you trapped in the void

allow yourself to grieve and surrender to its stages

rebirthing is not possible without accepting the death of

what you thought would be

the letting go is the most crucial part

the art of letting go before rebirth

the caterpillar knew what it meant to become a butterfly

it had turned itself into complete mush and surrendered itself to
the process

with acceptance and time

it transitions into an elegant butterfly

AWAY

floating through the clouds

is where you'll find me

I feel invisible here

away from my

human form

and all of the chaos

it feels liberating

but I must go back

and find myself

ANSWERS

you live in my dream state

away from reality

once my drowsy eyelids begin to shut

and the moon appears

you make your debut

searching for the answers

that I have yet to

unravel

we sit in silence

until dawn breaks

CPSIA information can be obtained
at www.ICGtesting.com
Printed in the USA
BVHW042214260722
643093BV00001B/10